Santa's Jet the Story!!!©

By Andrew P. And Diane M. Garcia

Copyright © 2010

ISBN: 979-8-9895766-5-4

Dedicated with much love,

for Ashlee, Julie, and Eric.

And now, also Ashton & Levi!

DISCLAIMERS

CONTENTS

Hi I'm Marty Moore,
Watch for me in Santa's Jet
ANIME
in 2024!!!

1-Introduction

AndyGarciaSounds LLC presents "Santa's Jet the Story"

.

by Andy and Diane Garcia

Read and sing the songs. Have Fun!

2-Sing the Song Jingle Bells

by James Pierpont – arr. Andrew P. Garcia ©

Verse 1

Dashing through the snow, in a one horse open sleigh

O'er the fields we go, laughing all the way

Bells on bob-tail ring, making spirits bright

What fun it is to ride and sing a sleighing song tonight

Chorus

Jingle bells, jingle bells, jingle all the way

Oh, what fun it is to ride in a one horse open sleigh, Hey!

Jingle bells, jingle bells, jingle all the way

Oh, what fun it is to ride in a one horse open sleigh

Verse 2

A day or two ago, I thought I'd take a ride

And soon Miss Fannie Bright, was seated by my side.

The horse was lean and lank, misfortune seemed his lot

He got into a drifted bank and we, we got upsot, oh… (chorus)

Verse 3

Now the ground is white, go it while you're young

Take the girls tonight, and sing this sleighing song

Just get a bobtailed bay, two forty for his speed

Then hitch him to an open sleigh and crack you'll take the lead (chorus)

3-No Dad for Christmas

Marty and Julie Moore were very sad. This would be their first Christmas ever without Dad. They had just moved from Juneau to Seattle so their mom, Ashlee, could start her new job. It was a great job with great pay, but the move was lousy timing. Their dad, Professor Ronald Moore, had to stay behind in Juneau and continue teaching and working in the Icefield Research Program through the end of the school year.

Marty and Julie had written to Santa Claus as soon as they found out Dad wouldn't be there for Christmas. "I'm sure Santa will help us," said six-year-old Julie. Julie had long brown hair like Mom and was always cheerful and a bit mischievous, which reflected in her big brown eyes. She adored her older brother, even when she thought he was being a pain!

Marty looked just like Dad with his blond hair and blue eyes and stood about a foot taller than Julie. Even though he loved his sister, he was almost nine, for heavens sakes, and didn't she know Santa might not be real?! "I'm not even sure there is a Santa," said Marty, with the tone that Julie knew meant he thought *he* was the smart one.

"Don't say that!" she said and smacked him on the arm. "If you say that, Santa will never help us see Dad for Christmas!"

"All right, but I'm gonna ask Mom if there's any way Dad can be here, just to be sure," said Marty.

"Don't do that either!" said Julie and hit his arm again. "You know Mom gets upset when we bring it up."

"I know, but we have to do something or we won't get to see Dad for Christmas!" said Marty.

Just then, Mom walked in. "What are you two talking about?" she asked.

"Oh nothing, Mom," said Marty. "I was just telling Julie she won't get anything for Christmas if she keeps hitting me on the arm." Julie threw a pillow at him.

"Julie!" Mom said. "Now you two get ready for bed."

"All right," they both said at the same time.

"Jinx!" said Julie. "You owe me a soda!" and she ran out of the room before Marty could say anything else.

4-Sing the song "Jolly Old St. Nicholas"

– USA – arr. Andrew P. Garcia©

Chorus

Jolly Old Saint Nicholas, lean your ear this way

Don't you tell a single soul, what I'm going to say

Christmas Eve will soon be here, now you dear old man

Whisper what you'll bring to me, tell me if you can.

Verse 1

When the clock is striking twelve, when I'm fast asleep

Down the chimney with your pack softly you will creep

All the stockings you will find, hanging in a row

Mine will be the shortest one, you'll be sure to know (chorus).

5-Alaska

Meanwhile, their dad, Ron, a tall thin man with a moustache and a warm smile, was talking to his boss, Sam, in his office in Juneau. Sam was a good man and Ron really liked having him as a boss. Sam stood about 6'3" tall and looked like he might have been a professional football player. "Sam, if I could just take a couple of days off to be with my kids for Christmas, it would mean so much to me! I'd be back before you know it!"

"I'm sorry, Ron, but you know we're at a very important part of the research monitoring and I've got five people out already due to the flu. We've gotta have you here. I promise once we're up to staff and past this point, I'll let you take time off to go visit your kids," Sam said. "I really am sorry."

What Ron really wanted to do was get mad at Sam, but Sam had always been good to him and now wasn't the time to complain.

"Talk about bad timing," Ron said under his breath as he left the room.

In another part of Alaska, the evil Professor Brett Beenie was plotting to keep Christmas from coming this year. Professor Beenie was a meanie. He was a short man with a round puffy face and small, beady eyes that appeared very large because of his big, horn rimmed glasses. Ever since he was five years old and didn't get an original Erector set with a small electric motor and pulleys, he stopped believing Santa Claus could deliver. He decided that if he didn't get what he wanted, nobody else would either! He swore that one day he would keep Christmas from coming at all. He'd worked long and hard to figure out where Santa's Village was and now he was ready to carry out his evil plan!

Professor Beenie had been busy working on a way to steal the power of flight from Santa's reindeer. He figured that if the reindeer couldn't fly, Santa wouldn't be able to deliver his presents, and if Santa couldn't deliver his presents, Christmas wouldn't come! Professor Beenie worked day and night and finally invented a potion using ionized crystals he called "Flight Robber". He even made the potion taste like Mrs. Claus's special oatmeal cookies, the reindeer's favorite food!

He was almost as excited to use the Flight Robber potion as he was the dimension shifter he'd created but never used. It looked just like a regular watch and no one would ever know it could actually get him into Santa's Village! His evil plan was to go to the North Pole and sneak the Flight Robber potion into the reindeer's food. Once the reindeer ate the potion, they wouldn't be able to fly. But that wasn't all! Then he'd wait and collect the reindeer droppings, put them through a careful cleaning process, and turn them into fuel for airplanes. He figured it only takes one reindeer dropping to power an airplane *forever*. He'd charge a fortune and not only would he stop Christmas, he'd make millions!

6- The North Pole

Up at the North Pole, Eric, Santa's Chief Scientist, Head of Development, and Chief of Security, burst into Santa's large cluttered office. Eric was small, even for an elf, but intelligence gleamed from his bright green eyes which were partially hidden by his long shaggy hair. "I've done it Santa, I've done it!"

"You've done what?" laughed Santa.

"I've invented a jet, powered by an electric solar powered super capacity battery! The jet's shiny silver with a convertible top and there's plenty of room for you, the presents, and even the reindeer. I'm calling it "Santa's Jet"!

"Now, Eric," Santa said, "why would I ever need a jet?" The reindeer have done a great job for centuries and our newest reindeer, Dancer, is proving to be every bit as good as her father Prancer, ever was!"

"I know Santa, but just in case. You always say we need a good back-up plan," said Eric, a little sad.

With his hands over his large belly, Santa chuckled, "Ho, ho, ho! I know Eric, but the reindeer have never, ever failed me." Seeing the disappointed look on the little elf's face, he said, "I'll tell you what. Let's take a look at what you've come up with. If something does happen, we'll have our back-up plan!"

Excitedly, Eric looked up and said, "Great – follow me!"

7- Christmas Eve

By late afternoon on Christmas Eve, Professor Beenie was ready to carry out his evil plan. Leaving a sled with its team of large, barking Huskies a short distance from the entrance to Santa's Village, he crept across the newly fallen snow, careful not to make too much noise as the snow crunched under his boots. Pressing a button on the dimension shifter he wore on his wrist, he watched as a frosty window appeared and he quickly climbed through. He spotted where the reindeer were housed and tiptoed his way inside, knowing Santa and the reindeer were probably having their final meeting in the main house before taking off for the night.

It was just as Professor Beenie had hoped! The feed bags were hanging full and ready for the reindeer to eat before their long night's flight. He pulled the potion from its pouch and uncorked the bottle. Quickly he poured a small amount into each feed bag, being careful not to spill a drop. He then ran quietly next door to the now silent workshop to wait. When the reindeer returned from the meeting with Santa, they were so hungry they went right to their feed bags. In no time at all, they had eaten all their food. Watching silently through the cracked doorway, Professor Beenie could hardly contain his evil laugh! He knew it was just a matter of time before the potion took effect.

Rudolph was the first to finish and left the stable to begin his take-off practice. The professor slipped out the side door and was just in time to see Rudolph crash into one of the giant Christmas trees!

"Nyah, ah, ah, it's working!" he cackled under his breath. Now all he had to do was wait for the potion to pass through the reindeer and collect the droppings for the fuel that would make him rich.

Back in Juneau, Ron was getting upset with his boss, Sam. "You want to drop me at the North Pole *today*?!" It's Christmas Eve!! What is so important that it can't wait?"   In a calm voice, Sam said, "I'm sorry Ron, but the monitor we posted up there a few months ago suddenly stopped working. Someone has to go check the equipment. If we lose the equipment, we'll probably lose our funding. We can't afford to take that chance."

"Why don't you do it?" Ron answered, not meaning to sound so angry with Sam.

Raising his voice slightly, Sam said, "Because I have to fly the chopper and you're the only one available who knows that equipment inside and out! Besides, after I drop you off, I have to go check to make sure there are no issues on the other end. We'll stay in radio contact and I'll come right back to get you once I make sure the connection is all right."

"Okay," said Ron fuming. "But you owe me – big time!"

8-Seattle

Back in Seattle, Marty and Julie were still worried about Dad being able to make it home for Christmas. They decided to talk to Mom, even if it upset her. "Mom, what if Santa didn't get our letter and Dad isn't here on Christmas day? We've never had a Christmas without all of us together!" Julie cried.

"Yeah, what's so important that they couldn't let him off for Christmas?" moaned Marty.

"Well," Mom said gently, "I'm sure you know how important Dad's work is and that what he's doing for the environment will affect everyone, right?"

"I guess," they both answered.

"Sometimes it just seems like he cares more about his job than he does about us," grumbled Marty.

"Oh Marty," she said, "You know that's not true! Your father is trying to make the world a better place to live, not just for you and Julie, but for your children and their children…action is so much more important than words and your dad's doing his part."

For a minute both children were silent.

"Does it help when I put my soda cans in the recycling bin?" asked Julie finally.

"Of course it does," she said, "Everyone can help by doing little things every day. But right now you two need to say your prayers and go to bed, Santa's coming tonight!"

"All right!" they both said at the same time.

"Jinx!" Julie said first. "You owe me a soda!"

"Oh man!" said Marty. "You always win! Well, g'nite mom, love you."

"I love you both so much!" she said kissing them both and scooting them off to bed.

9-Sing the song "Christmas Dream"

by Andrew P. Garcia©

Verse 1

Snow is lightly falling, peering from my room

All the gifts are open, this Christmas afternoon

And yet I have a dream, a dream of you and me

Of you and me together, this is my Christmas dream

Chorus

Christmas Dream, I never want to waken

Christmas Dream, don't leave me forsaken

Christmas Dream

Verse 2

Wanting you to hold me, take me in your arms

Having you, forever, what would be the harm

I love you, you love me, and yet we're far apart

My dream is to be together, if only in the heart (chorus)

10-Back at the Pole

Christmas Eve at the North Pole was now in full swing and it was getting closer to the time that Santa would need to leave to deliver the presents to the world. Santa was getting concerned that he hadn't seen the reindeer for a while and asked Eric to check on them.

Professor Beenie didn't have to wait long for the reindeer to do their "business". As soon as they were finished and headed toward the take-off site, he ran over to where they'd been and hurried to scoop the droppings out of the snow. It took a bag about the size of Santa's toy bag to hold all the droppings! He'd just turned around to push the button on his wrist when he saw one of Santa's security elves coming around the corner. He jumped back into the shadows and stood completely still until he thought the coast was clear. Tossing the heavy bag over his shoulder, he hurried and tiptoed back to the spot where he'd come through the dimension shifter and pushed the button on his wrist. As soon as the frosty window appeared, he slipped through.

Ron was just finishing the monitor repair inside the base tent and was putting a call through to Sam when he looked out and realized there was a dog sled team in the distance.

"That's odd," he thought. "What's someone doing up here tonight besides me?" Wondering where the person was who belonged to them, he decided to shoot a flare and see what happened. Just about the time he started to wonder if the person had anything to do with the damaged equipment, Sam's deep voice crackled over the radio. "Hey Sam," Ron said, "I've made the repairs and run a complete check on the equipment. She's all ready to go!"

"Good job!" Sam said. "I'm having some issues on my end, but should be able to pick you up by 10:00pm.

"Ten p.m.!" exclaimed Ron." That's three hours from now! It's not exactly warm out here!" The snow was now swirling in circles as it was being blown by the freezing wind.

"I'm sorry, Ron!" said Sam. "I'm doing everything I can to get to you as soon as possible. I don't like navigating in the night winds any more than you like being in the cold, but I need to make sure that we don't have to come back here because I missed something!"

"Understood," Ron sighed. "Oh, by the way, I saw a dog sled team a little ways away so I shot a flare to see what would happen. Just now I saw someone running toward the sled, but I have no idea where he came from."

"No kidding? Do you think he had anything to do with the broken equipment?"

"I wondered the same thing. I'll check it out while I'm waiting for you. Just don't take too long, please!"

"I'll hurry as fast as I can," Sam said as he hung up.

Professor Beenie had just stepped through the dimension shifter with the large bag of magic reindeer droppings when he saw the flare streaming into the sky. Afraid of getting caught and having to explain what he was doing there, he panicked and threw the bag back through the dimension shifter into Santa's Village.

He turned and ran as fast as he could to get to the sled. As he jumped on, he yelled, "Mush!" to the dog team and the Huskies bolted, jerking the sled and almost throwing him into a snowdrift. Professor Beenie held on for dear life as the sled sped away. As he got control of the sled, he started looking for a way to go back for the bag without being seen.

"Would you look at that," Ron said to himself. "I'd love to catch that guy and find out what he's up to. What's he doing up here, especially on Christmas Eve?"

In the meantime, Santa had assembled the elves in the large hall and was making final preparations to deliver presents.

"Ho, ho, ho!" laughed Santa as his eyes twinkled. "All right, folks, as soon as Eric gets back with the reindeer, we'll be ready to go!"

Zina, the tallest and thinnest of Santa's elves, came running up to Santa. She was

Santa's head elf of "Naughty and Nice" and "Present Fulfillment".

"Santa, Santa! What are you going to do about Julie and Marty seeing their dad for Christmas?"

"I'm sorry Zina," said Santa, "but you know my powers don't always work for things other than toys and games."

"But Santa," Zina said, "isn't there something you can do? Remember what happened with that boy, Brett Beenie, when he didn't get the erector set? He stopped believing and told all the other kids at school to stop believing too."

"I remember," said Santa. "That was the year his parents wrote to me and told me they wanted him to have a chemistry set instead of the Erector set. He never did get over that."

Santa seemed lost in thought for a moment. Suddenly coming back to the business at hand, he said, "But this is different, Zina. These children are asking me to deliver their *dad* for Christmas."

"I know, but I thought I'd at least find out where he is. I checked his office and found out they have him working in the field. They said he won't make it home by Christmas."

Santa said, "Well, keep doing what you can. I better get going or we'll have millions of disappointed children, not just those two."

"Okay, said Zina. "I'll keep working on it and let you know what I find out as soon as I can!"

As soon as Zina left, Eric came hurrying up to Santa. "Santa, Professor Beenie used his evil magic on the reindeer and now they can't fly! Christmas will be ruined!"

"Slow down, Eric! Catch your breath and tell me what's going on."

"I went to check on the reindeer and found them all really upset. They said they hadn't felt right since they ate and when they tried to practice their take-offs, they couldn't fly!! I was rushing back here to tell you when I saw someone leave the village so I checked the security cameras and saw that it was Brett Beenie. I think he did something to the reindeer!!"

"Oh my," Santa said as he stroked his long, white beard. "This is worrisome. Can any of them fly?"

"Not one of them!" said Eric, who was near tears.

Santa patted Eric on the back and laughed, "Ho, ho, ho, don't worry Eric. We'll use our number one back-up plan. Our jet – Santa's Jet!"

"But Santa," said Eric with some panic in his voice. "It's not quite ready!"

Thinking quickly, Santa said, "You take the elves from "Present Fulfillment, "and go finish the jet as fast as you can. I'll get the rest of the elves to help move the presents from the sled into the jet."

"All right!" said Eric. "I can't believe we're really gonna use it!"

11-Sing the song "Santa's Jet"

by Andrew P. Garcia©

Verse 1

Getting' fueled and ready to go

This ain't no time to take it slow

Kids across the world tonight

Will wake and scream out with delight

Chorus

'Cuz we're ridin' Santa's Jet

Yeah we're ridin' Santa's Jet

Well we're ridin' Santa's Jet

Yeah we're ridin' Santa's Jet across the world tonight

Verse 2

Here comes Rudolph, taking the lead

Dasher and Dancer runnin' up full speed

Mrs. Claus is wavin' goodbye

And that fat man Santa Claus is ready to fly (chorus)

Bridge

Watch out kids 'cuz he's ready to fly

He says he knows if you've been naughty or nice

You better be to sleep when he gets there

Or he'll say good-bye and leave your Christmas tree bare (chorus)

12- Jet Issues

Eric was so excited for Santa to be using his new invention, but very nervous that everything would go well.

"All right, Eric, I think it's time to start the engines!"

"Aye aye, Santa!"

Eric stepped over to the control panel and pressed the start button.

Nothing happened.

Eric laughed nervously and pressed the button again.

All was quiet….

Everyone gasped….

Nobody moved….

And then…

"It's not working!!" Eric yelled.

Frantically, Eric turned a few more knobs and pushed some more buttons.

"Okay, let's try it again!" he said with a hint of panic in his voice.

All was quiet….

Everyone gasped….

Nobody moved….

And then….the plane sputtered and coughed to life!

"It's working!! It's working!!" Eric said, jumping up and down excitedly.

The room erupted into cheers as Santa bent down and lifted Eric up onto his shoulders. They marched around the room with everyone joining the parade.

Suddenly everyone stopped. "The presents!!!" they yelled in unison. Working together with North Pole magic, the elves hurried and finished loading the bags of toys into the little jet. Next were the reindeer.

Santa carefully lifted Eric down from his shoulders, but held onto him in a big bear hug for just a minute longer.

"I'm so proud of you Eric. This is a fine jet! I'm curious, though – why is it so quiet?"

"Oh, I forgot to tell you! It's so high – tech, it's usually silent, but look…all you have to do is push this button and ….voila! A jet sound!!"

Santa smiled his biggest smile yet and said, "Great! We'll use the silent feature when we near the rooftops, but we can certainly use the jet sound everywhere else. Rudolph, are all the reindeer loaded?"

Rudolph nodded and flashed his bright, red nose. Santa climbed in last and buckled up. Once they were loaded and ready for take off, they looked just like the picture Eric had painted on the sides of the jet!

"Okay!! Is everyone ready? Now let's go!"

And off they went, just in the nick of time!

13- Sing the song "Up On the Housetop"

– Traditional arr. Andrew P. Garcia©

Verse 1

Up on the housetop reindeer pause

Out jumps good old Santa Claus

Down through the chimney with lots of toys

All for the little ones Christmas joys

Chorus

Ho, ho, ho who wouldn't go

Ho, ho, ho who wouldn't go oh

Up on the housetop click, click, click

Down through the chimney with good St. Nick

Verse 2

First comes the stocking of little Nell

Oh dear Santa fill it well

Give her a dolly that laughs and cries

One that can open and shut its eyes (chorus)

Verse 3

Look in the stocking of little Will

Oh just see what a glorious fill

Here is a hammer with lots of tacks

A whistle and a ball and a whip that cracks (chorus)

14- Pick Up

Just as Sam had promised, it was about 10:00pm when he arrived to pick up Ron. Ron held up a flare so that Sam could see where to land and he quickly hurried over to the helicopter as soon as Sam gave him the all-clear. They'd been lucky – the wind had let up and the glow from the Northern Lights made it easy to see, even that late at night.

"How did it go on your end?" Ron yelled to Sam over the loud whirring of the helicopter blades.

"Well it took longer than I wanted it to, but it's working great now," answered Sam.

"Awesome!" Ron said as he climbed in. "You know that guy I saw? I didn't even have a chance to get near him. Right after I shot up the flare, he jumped on the sled and took off. I guess we'll never know what he was doing up here or if he damaged the equipment."

"Hmm, I guess we'll have to leave it at that," said Sam. "Hopefully we won't have any more problems. And if all goes well, we should be home shortly after midnight."

"Home?" said Ron. "It's only home when I'm with my wife and kids."

"I'm sorry Ron," Sam said. "I *will* make it up to you next year."

"Right," Ron muttered, and they were silent the rest of the way home.

15- Saved the Day

Santa was able to deliver all the presents in record time! He thanked Eric over and over again for the fine back-up plan. "Eric, you really saved the day!" Santa said. "I didn't think we would ever use your invention, but we did and it was wonderful!"

"Thank you, Santa," Eric said beaming.

They walked together toward Santa's office as Eric explained what he'd found.

"While you were gone, I reviewed all the security cameras and saw that Professor Beenie had put something in the reindeer's food. I think that's what took away their ability to fly."

"How did he get in the village in the first place?" asked Santa. "We're checking into that right now, but we think it's something he's been working on ever since he was a young boy."

"Can anything be done to help the reindeer get their flight back?" said Santa.

"Yes," replied Eric enthusiastically. "I also noticed that when he went to leave, a man we'd seen up here doing some repairs fired a flare. It must have scared him so he threw a bag back through some kind of "window" and took off. I sent security to pick it up and it ended up being reindeer droppings..."

"*Reindeer droppings*?!" exclaimed Santa.

"I know – strange, huh?! Anyway, I took it to the lab and we were able to figure out what he did. He put an ionized crystal solution in the feed that absorbed their power of flight. We think he planned to use the crystals from the droppings to power who-knows-what for magical flight. The lab separated the crystals from the droppings and put them through a sanitizer. Now all we have to do is mix them in water, pour a little in to the feed bags and they should be able to fly again!"

"Ho, ho, ho!" laughed Santa. "Great job, Eric! I think the reindeer enjoyed the jet ride, but I think they'd be much happier using their own magical powers of flight."

"I agree, Santa," Zina interrupted. She had just returned from the reindeer's quarters. "By the way, I had the backup elves deliver a special present to Julie and Marty's dad. I just hope he opens it in time!"

"Good work, Zina," said Santa.

"Santa, what are you going to do about the evil Professor Beenie?" Eric asked.

"Well, Eric," said Santa, "When Brett Beenie didn't get the toy he wanted, he got so angry that he wanted to ruin Christmas for everyone. That's why he tried to stop us tonight. But I believe it's never too late to bring a little joy into someone's life, so I delivered that toy to him tonight. I think it just might soften his heart a little."

Eric said, "All right, but just in case it doesn't change his attitude, I'll make sure Santa's jet is always ready!"

"Ho, ho, ho," laughed Santa, "just in case!"

16- Merry Christmas

Professor Beenie couldn't believe his plan had been foiled! All those years of planning and work down the drain! Those interfering little elves had grabbed the bag of reindeer droppings just as he was sneaking back in to get it. He was furious!

Now, here he was, back again on the outskirts of town. It just made him feel even more depressed and angry than he already was to come back to the same old boring place. He never decorated his house for the Christmas season – or any other holiday for that matter – and his place looked lifeless compared to everyone else's.

He reached his porch and unlocked the front door, but before stepping inside, he turned and shook his fist at the sky and yelled, "I'll get you Santa! You won this year, but I *will* stop Christmas from coming!!" He slammed the door behind him, turned around, and froze.

Was he seeing things? He hadn't put up a Christmas tree. He rubbed his eyes and looked again. Sure enough, there in the center of the living room stood a beautiful little pine decorated with shiny gold ornaments. He stood frozen to the spot, trying to make sense of what he was seeing. It was then that he realized there was something under the tree.

Slowly and carefully, he started making his way across the room. He still couldn't believe what he was seeing and even though he was very curious, he had to admit he was a little afraid of the sight before his eyes. Still….something was drawing him closer and closer

That couldn't be. A red case? As the memories began to stir, he took a few steps closer to the little tree and the mystery beneath it. Now he could see the pictures on top of the case. This wasn't happening. It must be a dream! He pinched himself hard on the arm and yelped in pain. Two more steps and he was able to reach out and touch the case. It *was* real! It was the original Erector set with pulleys and a small electric motor that he had wanted for Christmas when he was a child!

He dropped to the floor and pulled the red case onto his lap, suddenly feeling like a little boy again. He didn't quite know what to think. For years he'd tried to buy just this set but it was no longer sold in the stores and he'd given up hope of ever having his wish come true. He'd become so angry inside and was so tired of being unhappy.

Somewhere inside he realized this was his own little miracle. He suddenly felt ashamed of all the wasted time he'd spent trying to get back at Santa and the rest of the world. He knew that it was time to make things right – Santa had come through after all! For now though, he had a toy to play with…..

Ron got back to his apartment much later than he'd hoped, but he was glad he'd at least set up a small, artificial tree on the coffee table. His family had left it behind for him to use this Christmas and he didn't want to disappoint them.

He was in a grumpy mood, especially when he realized it was already Christmas morning now and not Christmas Eve. He'd thought it might work out for him to be with his wife and kids for the holidays. Instead, here he was, all alone in this small apartment.

He set down all his gear and plopped on the couch, very tired and very sad. He really didn't feel like getting up again and didn't care if he turned on the lights to the little tree, but he kept thinking about his family and how much he missed them. Since he knew it would make them sad to know he had no Christmas spirit, he decided to get up after all and cheer the place up while he had a quick bite to eat.

As he headed into the kitchen, he paused at the little Christmas tree and plugged in the lights. A red and green glow lit up the room and he was surprised when he realized it *did* make him feel better. He turned to continue into the kitchen and did a double-take when he realized there was a large, gold envelope under the tree that wasn't there when he'd left that morning.

He glanced around the room, half expecting to see his family there to surprise him, but it was perfectly quiet and he was sure he was alone in the apartment. He reached out and picked up the envelope, seeing for the first time that someone had written in large red letters the words "Merry Christmas Ronald!"

"Who in the world…?" he thought. No one had called him Ronald since he was a young boy. Hurriedly he slit open the envelope and pulled out the papers from inside. His mouth opened wide in surprise as he realized it was a plane ticket for the early flight leaving Juneau to Seattle – in a few hours! He picked up his cell phone and dialed Sam.

"Hey, Sam! Sorry if I woke you, but thanks so much for the plane ticket. I'm surprised you took a chance that we'd be done!"

"What are you talking about?" asked Sam, yawning. "What plane ticket?"

"When I got back to my apartment, there was an envelope under my little Christmas tree with a plane ticket to Seattle. I just figured it had to be from you!"

"It isn't from me. Maybe it's from your wife and kids," Sam said.

Ron thought about that for a moment and then said, "No, somehow I'm just sure they had nothing to do with it. But if they didn't and you didn't, then who did?"

"I don't know, but since we're up and running and Ben Holstead let me know he's ready to come back, I think we can afford to have you leave. Go have Christmas with your family, Ron! And if you do find out who left you the ticket, let me know!"

"I will Sam. Have a Merry Christmas – see you when I get back!"

"Merry Christmas to you too, Ron!"

Ron hung up the phone and didn't know what to do first. He couldn't believe this was happening! He was so excited he started jumping and dancing around the room. Realizing he was no longer tired, he decided to put on some Christmas music and start packing for the flight – after all, it was leaving in a few hours!

He considered calling his wife to let her know he was coming, but decided he didn't want to wake them. Besides, this way he could surprise them. He felt so blessed – he was going to be home for Christmas after all!

17- Surprise

In Seattle, it was still dark when Marty and Julie crept into Mom's room to see if she was awake. They were as quiet as could be, but since moms have radar when it comes to their children, she heard them before they got to the bedside.

"What are you two doing up already?" Mom said wearily.

"Sorry, Mom, but we just couldn't sleep anymore! We're too excited!" Marty answered.

Mom couldn't really sleep anymore either since she was a little sadder about Dad being gone for Christmas than she wanted Julie and Marty to know. She wanted them to enjoy Christmas as much as they could without Dad, so she yawned and stretched and threw off the covers to climb out of bed.

"You two stay here for just a minute while I check on things," Mom said.

"Aw, Mom, do we have to?" whined Julie.

"Yes," Mom said. "I'll only be a minute, sweetie," as she kissed first Julie and then Marty on the forehead. The house was still chilly so she put on her robe and slippers and headed downstairs to the living room to flip on the switch for the gas fireplace.

She took a look around the room and was glad to realize she was feeling a little like a child herself, wanting very much to open her presents, too! She kept reminding herself that even without Dad here on Christmas morning, they had a lot to be grateful for.

"Okay, you two – come on down!" yelled Mom.

Sounding like a herd of elephants, Marty and Julie raced down the stairs and into the living room. Wide-eyed with wonder, they ran to the tree and started sorting through the gifts to find the ones bearing their names. They took each of the presents they'd wrapped for Mom and set them on the couch next to where she was sitting. Then they sat down on the floor and began taking turns unwrapping their gifts.

"An e-pad?! Cool!" exclaimed Marty.

Mom opened the gifts Marty and Julie had made for her and had to hide the sudden tears at the corners of her eyes. She knew they'd made gifts for Dad, too, but she didn't know when he'd be home to open them. "I love you guys so much!" was all she could muster.

"Once Dad finally moves here for good, it'll be so much fun!" Marty said and then it suddenly became quiet. "I miss Dad," Marty finally said.

"I do too," said Julie sounding like she might start to cry. Mom hurried and said, "We all do, but we can call him later and wish him a Merry Christmas. Now, come over here – we need a group hug!"

After they finished opening their gifts, they headed toward the kitchen to start making breakfast, but decided to call Dad first.

Just then, the phone rang, and Julie and Marty raced to answer it, but Marty beat her by just a hair.

"Hello?"

"Merry Christmas, son!" sang Dad

"Dad! We were just going to call you – Merry Christmas to you, too!"

Julie was tugging at Marty's arm trying to grab the phone from him. "I want to talk to him, too!" she said.

Marty bent over so that Julie could put her ear up to the phone at the same time.

"Have you opened the presents yet?" asked Dad. "We just finished. We got a game, Dad!" exclaimed Julie.

"Great! That'll be fun to play together, won't it?!"

"Except we don't know when you'll be home to try it!" said Marty.

Mom had walked over to where they were standing talking on the phone to Dad when they heard a knock at the front door. They all looked at each other, wondering who it could be.

"Hang on a sec, Dad. Someone's at the front door," said Marty.

"Who would be knocking at the door on Christmas morning?" Mom said as she walked over to answer it, Marty and Julie on her heels.

They flung it open and there stood Dad!

"Dad!" they both yelled at the same time.

"Jinx!" Marty said. "You owe me a soda!"

"I don't care," Julie said, "'cuz Dad's here! I knew there was a Santa!"

"There must be, Julie," Dad said, "because we're all here and one big happy family! Let's dance for joy! Mom, throw on some music!"

18- Sing the Song "Santa Calypso"

by Andrew P. Garcia©

Verse 1

Christmas day is the time to play, when all of Santa's work is done

Elves, reindeer and Christmas cheer, run rampant 'til the evenin' sun

Chorus

They do the Santa calypso, and Santa will lead

They do the Santa calypso, it's just what we need

They do the Santa calypso, it's time to have fun

They do the Santa calypso, for everyone

Verse 2

They all join hands to follow the band, and Santa is the talk of the town

He says, "Shuffle right and then shuffle left, shake your belly turn left one fourth around, that's it! (chorus)

Bridge

All right everybody, it's time to do the Santa calypso, ready, let's go

Step left right left, then right left right

Grapevine left, grapevine right

Shuffle right, shuffle left

Shake your belly turn left one fourth around, that's it! (chorus)

Verse 3

He wiggles his belly like a bowl full of jelly

His laugh really says, "Ho, ho, ho!"

He's happy for you, this Christmas is through

Next Christmas everybody gets more

(chorus)

19- Author's Note:

The Christmas story began with the birth of Jesus, born in a manger to loving, earthly parents who were there to protect him on his journey through life. Christmas became a time for family and friends to show their love for one another through sharing, caring and giving. With that thought in mind, we would like to close with this song which is the true reason we celebrate Christmas.

20- Sing the song "What Child is This?"

by William C. Dix (arr. Andrew P. Garcia©)

Verse 1

What child is this, who laid to rest, on Mary's lap is sleeping

Whom angels greet with anthems sweet

While shepherds watch are keeping (chorus)

Chorus

This, this is Christ the King

Whom shepherds guard and angels sing

Haste, haste to bring him laud

The babe, the son of Mary

Verse 2

So bring him incense, gold and myrrh

Come peasant king to own Him

The King of Kings, salvation brings

Let loving hearts enthrone him (chorus)

The End

CREDITS

Written by Andy and Diane Garcia

Edited by Jenny Swisher and Diane Garcia

Cover and back Illustrations by Courtlynn Johnson

Inside Illustrations by Julie A. Garcia

Santa's Jet the Story is published by Andrew P. Garcia dba AndyGarciaSounds LLC. Copyright ©2010 by Andrew P. Garcia dba AndyGarciaSounds LLC. All rights reserved.

Music by Andrew P. Garcia dba
AndyGarciaSounds LLC Copyrights: -
-Santa's Jet ©1989.
-Jolly Old Saint Nicholas ©2009
-Up On the Housetop ©2009.
-Christmas Dream ©1989.
-Santa Calypso ©2008.
-Jingle Bells ©2009.
-What Child is This ©2009

About the Authors:

Andy and Diane Garcia are from Utah and have been together since 1989. That's when Andy wrote the song "Santa's Jet" and started working on the story. With the demands of supporting a family taking priority, efforts to finish the book took longer than expected. The first draft of the book was finally finished in 2009 and they were able to obtain the copyrights in 2010.

In 2019, they started Santa's Jet in Anime form which was completed in 2023. Publishing is anticipated to be in 2024.

Andy and Diane would like to thank everyone who inspired and contributed to making this story possible. They have read this to their children and grandchild and and have a lot of fun singing the songs with them as well! It is their hope that this will become a Christmas tradition for your family as it has with theirs. Please enjoy and have fun!

Please visit our website:
santasjetplus.com or scan QR code.